Gaymers

by

Zahra Jons

This is a work of fiction.
Names, characters, businesses, places, events,
or incidents are either the products of the
author's imagination or used in a fictitious
manner. Any resemblance to actual person,
living or dead, or actual events is purely
coincidental.

CHAPTER 1

The new gaming system was always plugged into the flat screen, ready to play whatever game Aiden was in the mood for. He didn't use it as often as he used to; the online games were littered with kids in it to win, and he'd rather play for the fun and adventure.

The older box—a gift on his fourteenth birthday—was still usable and connected to a switch box that also connected the Blu-Ray player. It needed a lot more connectors and an adaptor to work with the newer TV, but he never completely unplugged it.

He flipped the switch and tapped the "on" button, watching the old graphics come into slow focus on the screen. It was late; he wasn't going to play, but he needed to see the names come up for the game that would never be finished.

Ayy-den

Stu-doo

Con-noob

Stu hadn't really played the game the way Aiden and Connor had, but the two had kept his avatar going, taking turns playing his character when necessary. That way, when Stu was over, and not at football practice, they could all play together—unless Stu's avatar died, which was a frequent occurrence when it was Stu playing.

Aiden stared at the blinking names, his focus blurring. He missed Connor. Wished with everything in him that he knew where he was, that he was okay. Seeing him again would be both heartbreaking and a relief at the same time.

Do you want to continue the adventure?

He picked up a controller and tapped for "no". It was time to go to bed. If he stayed up too much longer, he'd put himself into a funk and his mother would be able to tell in the morning and ask questions.

CHAPTER 2

"I hate you!"

Aiden woke at the words, not spoken aloud, except in his dream. They hadn't been spoken in reality at any time, even though most of the dream was memory.

His sigh heavy, he pushed back the comforter—he never bothered with a sheet, even in his parents' house, his sleep could be so restless it wound up on the floor—and stood. The dream always started with happier memories, playing video games, eating ice cream and pizza, and then the kissing...which quickly evaporated into a nightmare where CPS busted in and dragged Connor away.

That's not what happened. Not really. Child Protection arrived on a Saturday morning at his friend's house in the mobile home park and took him away, but he hadn't been dragged and he hadn't screamed. He'd looked betrayed, tears streaking his face, his mother sobbing on the front step of the old trailer, his father swaying boozily against the dilapidated railing, yelling obscenities, a police officer restraining him.

Connor would hate him if he knew he'd been the one to call and report his dad.

Of course, he'd not been the only one calling CPS. Mrs. Wilson, an elderly woman who'd lived two lots down in the park, had also called several times to report the yelling and that Connor's mom often sported bruises. But no one had ever responded to her calls.

The woman had passed away a couple years ago, the whole town thinking she'd been the one to finally turn the man in. But they were wrong.

Aiden thought about Connor a lot. More than he should. Or maybe, it was just more than he wanted.

Stretching, pulling on an old sweatshirt over his bare chest and black pajama bottoms, he climbed the stairs from the basement to his parents' kitchen and started the coffee. He was home for a weeklong vacation—it was the start of Spring Break and Stu's 23rd birthday weekend and Elias' 4th. No way would he miss those celebrations, even if there wouldn't be beer on the menu. And then Dad wanted help with putting new windows in the garage, so he'd taken time off to help.

Maybe the dream was because he was home. The three of them—Aiden, Connor, and Stu—had spent many a winter weekend in the basement playing video games, watching movies, and eating whatever food was brought down to them. That had all changed a couple of days after Aiden's 17th birthday, when Connor had been taken away.

His friend had only been 15 (almost 16) and had given Aiden an unforgettable birthday present: a first kiss. It had gone a bit more than that, but not far, Connor's face tinging bright pink when they'd broken apart.

It had been wonderful, though, until somehow, Connor's dad had found out and threatened Aiden—and Connor. He'd told Aiden what he planned to do with his faggot son.

Aiden had been terrified for his friend—and had placed that irretrievable phone call.

CHAPTER 3

"You look rough." Aiden's dad came down the stairs from the second floor of the 1970s-built split-level.

"Yeah," Aiden cleared the toad from his throat, "bad dreams."

His dad said nothing more, just pulled a couple of mugs from the cupboard and set them on the counter next to the coffee maker. The rush of water from the faucet filled the kitchen for the minute or so it took to fill the glass carafe and pour it into the reservoir.

It was a comfortable quiet, the only sound the gurgle of water running though the machine to come out an aromatic brew.

Aiden squinted at a car that turned into the drive. It was an old Ford Pinto, its green paint accentuated by rust. He didn't recognize it. "Dad, do you know that car?"

His dad joined him at the window, pulling his glasses from the top of his head to his nose.

"It has New York plates."

"Huh." His dad tilted his head to get a better look. "No."

The headlights turned off and the car's engine stopped, but the driver didn't get out. It was still dim out, the sun not quite over the horizon, and it was hard to see through the porch light reflected on the windshield.

The coffee finished and Dad poured coffee into the two mugs and pulled another from the cupboard. "Just in case."

Aiden didn't respond.

The driver opened their door and stood, and there was no mistaking who it was. No matter that a little less than five years had passed.

His breath caught in his throat.

The driver was taller than Aiden's memories, which made sense. And he was heavier—he'd been pretty scrawny as a kid and teenager—but it looked good on him. The curly hair was a little darker, and shorter, and Aiden knew that when he'd made it into the light, he'd have bottle-green eyes and a pouty bottom lip.

"Connor."

He wasn't aware that he'd spoken aloud until his dad asked, "Hmm? What about him? You haven't talked about him for a while."

Aiden straightened from his slouch into the countertop. "He's here. That's him in the Pinto."

"What?" Dad came back to the window, craning his neck a little to see where the young man had walked to the front door and stood, staring at the doorbell, hand raised but not quite ready to press the glowing button. "I'll go let him in."

Aiden couldn't move. He wanted to run and jump and yell, but wasn't sure if it was out of fear or joy. His friend was back, but he wasn't sure why.

CHAPTER 4

Mom came down at the sound of all the voices and squealed and hugged Connor, kissing both of his cheeks and hugging him again.

Connor looked like he wasn't sure what to do, but endured the onslaught of affection without complaint.

"Miriam, let the boy breathe." Dad chuckled but wrapped an arm around her to keep her from going into smother mode again.

"It's just..." she choked up and wiped tears from her eyes, "I've been so worried for so long. No one would tell us anything about where you were or how you were doing."

Connor shrugged and nodded. "Yeah. There's some rule that they can't tell you anything in case you'd tell my parents." He licked his lips. "I don't think any of you ever would, but I guess CPS doesn't trust anyone."

"Well," Mom clapped her hands and offered a teary laugh, "At least you're home now, and that's what's important. Just in time for Stu's birthday!" She made herself busy at the fridge, grabbing bacon and eggs and butter. "Everyone sit and enjoy your coffee while I make breakfast."

Dad poured a cup for Connor, retrieving the carton of creamer from the fridge and setting it next to the sugar bowl in the center of the table.

Aiden sat, spooning three heaps of sugar into his cup. Connor sat next to him, adding creamer and sugar to his.

Grinning, Dad took a long drag of plain black coffee. "Wimps." He smacked his lips.

13

"We just still have our taste buds." Aiden's equilibrium was returning and he felt capable of quipping back to his dad, though he thought his voice may have cracked a bit. No one seemed to notice, or at least were polite enough not to say anything.

"You still like bacon, Connor?" Mom spoke from the stove, where she was laying thick strips on the broiler.

Connor swallowed a mouthful of coffee. "Yes, ma'am."

Mom grinned and added more bacon to the broiler. She was always happy feeding people, and Connor was no exception, other than she might get particularly more joy out of it than usual. She always made him a special dinner for his birthday, just like she had done for her own children.

"So," Dad leaned forward, "do we spring him on Stu or give him a head's up?"

Aiden blinked. "I think we need to tell him."

Dad nodded. "Okay." And stood to walk to the phone.

Glancing at the kitchen clock, Aiden chuckled. "You might want to give him a chance to wake up first. It's not even half-past seven."

"Ah, right, right." Instead of wandering back to the table, Dad went to the toaster and bread box. "You ready for me to start making the toast?"

"Yes, dear." Miriam nodded and set two over-easy eggs on a plate. "Your eggs are done. How do you like your eggs, Connor? Still hard over?"

"Yes, please."

CHAPTER 5

It was strange, having Connor there, the conversation so much like those from the past. It was like déjà vu, but not, because Connor was older, his voice deeper, more confident than when he'd been a kid.

The wafting aroma of smoky bacon filled the kitchen. "Ken, here—put this on a plate, please. The tongs are in the drawer." Mom waved vaguely at the drawers next to the dishwasher.

Dad found the tongs and set the bacon on a towel-lined platter to drain, setting three of the crispiest strips on his own plate. He grinned and winked at those at the table. "Benefits of being the helper."

Connor laughed, the sound natural and relaxed.

16

Aiden didn't think it fair how easy Connor was acting; Aiden thought his stomach might jump out his throat and rumba around the room if he said too much. He was conscious of his ratty sweatshirt—there was a hole on one side where the seam had pulled out and paint stains from the last time he'd helped his dad paint the shed. His awareness spread to the fact that he wore his oldest pair of pajama bottoms; he might have had them before Connor left.

Dad set his and Connor's plates on the table. "Mom's making you scrambled eggs now, Aiden."

"No rush." He lifted his coffee cup. "I'm still on my first cup." It was normal for him to have nothing for breakfast but coffee during the school week, and sleep in until almost noon on the weekends so he'd only eat dinner. It was different here in his parents' house—the home of his childhood—where old routines came back and he never really slept in.

The jangle of the phone startled everyone; Aiden almost lost his breakfast to the kitchen floor, but Mom recovered and balanced his plate just in time.

He took it from her and set it on the table, watching his dad answer the call.

"'morning." His dad rocked on his heels and laughed. "Sure, Stu. You and Elias can come over now." He held the phone away from his ear then set it back. "I guess he's excited about the party, eh?"

Aiden couldn't hear Stu's reply, which wasn't unusual. Stu was soft-spoken and perpetually calm; it surprised a lot of folks who'd expected him to play pro-football.

"Ah, Stephanie had to work an extra half-shift last night. No, no problem. Only..." Dad glanced to the table, "there's a surprise someone here."

There was quiet while Dad listened to Stu. "No, I don't think I'll tell you who, since you're coming over early so you can get it all out of your system before the party starts." More quiet, followed by a soft chuckle from Dad. "No, you can't wheedle it out of me. If you hurry, Miriam can make you breakfast."

Dad nodded and hug up the phone, turning to smile at Mom. "Elias wants scrambled eggs with cheese, please." He wagged a finger. "No onion."

Aiden snickered. That was Elias' thing now, to ask for everything without onions after he'd gotten something with big chunks of the vegetable in it. The little boy would even ask for ice cream without onions.

"Poor thing. That church casserole traumatized him." Mom started whipping a couple more eggs for the frying pan.

Right. Mrs. Shannon's breakfast casserole at Easter breakfast was the culprit. Aiden couldn't really blame Elias; there had been big chunks of green pepper in there, too, but they were easier to pick out.

"I'll put a fresh pot of coffee on." Dad poured the already-made brew into a bottle and set it in the fridge to make iced coffee later, humming while he scooped out the grounds and filled the pot with water.

CHAPTER 6

It took all of five minutes—the coffee was still dripping—for Stu to arrive. The young family only lived a couple of blocks over, in one of the new apartment buildings, though Aiden knew that it could take an hour if Elias was fussy and non-cooperative. The tyke must really want those eggs and cheese.

"Holy shit!" Stu stood in the door to the kitchen—he never bothered ringing the bell, this was his second home—his young son in his arms staring at his face.

"Daa," the little boy leaned close to whisper loudly into this father's ear, "you said a bad word. I'm telling Momma that you said it in front of me."

But Stu wasn't really listening and didn't even protest when Aiden walked around the table to take his godson from his arms. "C'mere, you. I think your dad can be forgiven this once."

Connor stood, too, hands shoved in his pockets, a light pink flushing his cheeks. "Hey, Stu. Long time no see and all that."

"Mother fu-"

"Hey!" Mom slapped the counter. "That is not a forgivable word, even under these circumstances."

Stu blinked and looked sheepish. "'I'm sorry, Mrs. McDougall. I forgot myself there. But...Connor?"

"Yup, all day long." Connor winced and the pink in his cheeks darkened.

Elias guffawed. "That's funny."

If Aiden wasn't used to the way the little boy squirmed when he laughed, he might have dropped him, but he knew and let him fake-slip through his arms only to catch him up again.

That only made the toddler laugh and squirm even harder.

"Aiden, stop that. You'll make him sick before he even gets to eat his eggs." Mom's reprimand didn't sound angry, and she set a bowl of cooled scrambled eggs and melted cheese on the table. "Grab the booster so he can eat."

It was Stu who grabbed the wooden riser and strapped it to the chair for his son while Aiden tickled the little boy so that tears streamed down his cheeks.

Mom sighed and shook her head, but didn't bother saying anything this time.

Elias squirmed in the booster, but a soft word whispered in his ear from his dad had him settling down to his eggs and a sippy cup of milk. Stu sat next to him to monitor his progress, containing the little-boy mess as best he could.

"Were we this bad when we were this age?" Stu wiped cheese and milk from his son's tennis shoe.

"Worse." Mom set a plate of eggs and toast in front of Stu. "Much, much worse."

Aiden watched; it was better than watching Connor, though he would have preferred to just sit and observe him all day long. His forearms were muscled, sleek with a faint smattering of blond hair, and his jaw held a bit of stubble he'd missed shaving that morning. His curls cupped his ears just as they always had.

He was hot and sexy, and Aiden wasn't sure how to react. Certainly not the way he wanted—especially not in front of his parents and Stu and Elias.

Oh, they knew he liked men; he'd even brought a boyfriend—Jason Bartel—home during spring break his freshman year of college that might have worked out but...Jason had wanted more than Aiden could give him at the time. It was a

24

mostly amicable break-up.

Except for the fight about the old gaming system. Jason had told Aiden to throw it away if he wasn't using it anymore—and Aiden had explained that he still used it sometimes—and Jason's reply had been enough for Aiden to tell him to leave. There had been shouting— again, more about the system than their relationship—and he'd left.

Aiden had been relieved; which, when he'd eventually been honest with himself, said more about that relationship than anything else.

He'd talked to his mom about the fight and the game system and his relief that Jason was no longer in his life. His mother had smiled and rubbed his back and told him that sometimes relationships weren't meant to last forever, that they were learning opportunities to help you find what you need and want in a partner.

But he'd never talked to anyone about that seventeenth birthday kiss; not Stu, not his mom, not even his dad, who'd been the first to figure out he was gay and tell him it was okay.

CHAPTER 7

Three hours later, Stephanie arrived, yawning and sleepy from her extra-long practicum shift in ICU, but with the rolls and birthday cake from the bakery. Not Holstein's Bakery—they didn't like to bake for gays, so Mom and Dad wouldn't buy from them anymore, and Stu and Stephanie agreed—but from Sheila-Mae's Sweet Shoppe. It was new and the owner from away, but she'd stick a rainbow unicorn on anything without batting a fake eyelash and give you a discount just because.

They were all in the basement family room watching the ending of Shrek—Elias was dancing to the final song—when Stephanie called down the stairs. "I'm here! Are you?"

"Hey," Stu called back, not rising

27

from the floor where he sat—Elias had been on his lap most of the movie, "come on down."

The stairs barely creaked when the petite young woman came down. Sometimes, seeing her standing beside her hulking six-five former high-school football-player husband was jarring; photos could look photoshopped, and more than once Aiden had been accused of doing just that until the person had met the couple in person.

When she reached the bottom, with Elias shrieking like he hadn't seen his mother in weeks rather than just a few hours, it took her a few minutes to realize there was someone new in the room.

"Oh, hello." She smiled around her son's butting head.

"Hi." Connor waved from the sofa.

Elias puffed out his chest. "That's Dad-and-Uncle-Aiden's-friend Connor from back when they were in hai ska-ool." He leaned close to her ear. "Dad swear-d-ed when he saw him."

Stephanie stared a long moment, just blinking. Then..."You're Connor?"

Elias giggled. "Yup, he is. All day long." And then guffawed in his mother's face.

Connor groaned and covered his face. "I am so sorry."

Stu also groaned, but it was followed by a good-natured arm punch. "Don't worry, Connor, you'll pay long and dearly for that every time someone introduces you."

Aiden snickered. "At least he didn't say without onions."

Which immediately prompted the little boy to shout, "and he came without onions!"

CHAPTER 8

The party progressed without incident, and the guests—consisting of a mix of Stu's friends and their children—didn't bat an eye at Connor's attendance. James and Pat didn't remember him from high school, having graduated before Aiden and Stu, and Billie and Janice were new to the area and didn't know the history of the trio. And the kids—Jaden, James' son, and Alicia, Billie and Janice's daughter, didn't care—they just wanted to play with Elias.

By the end, Aiden just wanted it to be over. He wanted Connor to himself, so they could talk and catch up and maybe...well, that wasn't likely to happen, so he'd just accept talking and catching up.

He'd even be okay with Stu being

there, after all, the three of them had done pretty much everything together after the day high-schoolers Aiden and Stu had decided to walk what they thought was a picked-on elementary school kid to school and found out he was in the seventh grade.

St. Barnaby was a small town, and didn't have a separate middle school, so the elementary school went up to sixth grade, in the old high school building, with seventh grade and up all going to the new high school building, though the grades were split into separate wings. They shared a library, cafeteria, and gymnasium, though the high school programs had gotten first dibs on any of those spaces for extra-curricular events.

Now, with the influx of new families, the elementary school went through eighth grade in what used to be the new high school, while nine through twelve attended in an even newer building on the

31

edge of town, where it got a new football field and gymnasium complex.

What had once been the high school, then the elementary school, now housed the pre-K and kindergarten programs and the administrative offices.

Aiden was very familiar with the politics of the school system of St. Barnaby—his father had been the high school principal through his graduation, then moved to assistant superintendent for a couple of years before retiring. He still sat on the PTA board in an emeritus status.

His mother had been an elementary school teacher before having children, and then run a private child development center until the system had started the formal pre-elementary program. She'd been more or less out of a job then, but had made the best of it by staying home and becoming a children's book author.

That his mother had a famous pen name never ceased to amaze Aiden. That so many folx in town knew nothing about it amazed him even more.

With Elias asleep on her shoulder, Stephanie smiled at her husband and patted his shoulder. "I can handle our spawn for a couple hours. Hang around and catch up with your friend. I know you want to." She headed out the side gate to the paved driveway.

Stu looked sheepish, and followed, Aiden and Connor tagging along. "Yeah, I do. But..."

"Plans change, hon. It's okay." And she stretched up her face, puckering her lips for a kiss.

Which she got when her husband bent down. "Thank you. I might not be invited, you know."

His wife snorted and turned away. "Yeah, right."

33

Aiden laughed. "She's correct. You know you're always welcome here."

"Yeah, but one day she'll use that against me by knowing she can kick me out and I'll have somewhere to go." Stu waved and laughed when his wife raised a middle finger in his direction.

"One day, the kid's gong to see that." Stu wagged a finger.

Stephanie ignored him and strapped their son into the car seat. "I'll see you when you get home. Ask for a ride if you have more than a couple beers."

"I will." Stu waved again.

Aiden leaned against the wooden fence, Connor just beside him holding the gate open. He was painfully aware of him being so close, and only hoped Stu couldn't tell. That wasn't a conversation he wanted to have yet—ever, if he could help it. Unless...but that was wishful thinking and wishes didn't always come

34

true.

He led the other two into the house through the side door of the garage.

"Are you three going to hang out in the basement?" Mom was putting away leftover cake, rolls, steak, and macaroni salad in the kitchen.

"Probably." Aiden shrugged; that had always been their hangout spot of choice.

"Dad and I are going out for our monthly dinner club. It should have been last Saturday but it got postponed when Carmella Montgomery's daughter had the baby." Mom twisted plastic wrap around the rolls before setting them in the bread box. "Aiden, you know where everything is; Stu, so do you. Connor, just ask. If you drink, take out the bottles; I don't clean up after that. Dirty dishes go in the dishwasher; start it if its full."

Mom turned to glare at each of

them in turn. "The rules haven't changed."

"Yes, ma'am." The three chorused in unison.

It was so much like old times.

She nodded and started up the stairs. "We'll be out of here in half an hour. Aiden, you know our cell numbers if you need us."

"Mom, I'm 21—almost 22. I'm not a kid."

"I know, I know, but you'll always be my child." And she disappeared.

Aiden shrugged at his friends. "What are ya gonna do?"

Stu snickered. "Call your mother if something happens."

Groaning, Aiden led the way to the basement. "Nothing is going to happen that I'll want to tell her about."

Connor laughed, the sound low and

throaty, and it made Aiden's stomach-butterflies dance.

CHAPTER 9

They played a game on the new game box, a fantasy adventure that Aiden liked and wasn't too embarrassed to play in front of his mother or father if they came down to the basement. It wasn't overly long, with the adventures only taking an hour or so to play, depending on how you played and with whom.

He and Stu had tried to play it with Elias one rainy Saturday afternoon last summer; it hadn't gone well when the toddler hadn't been able to operate the buttons. Stu had wound up playing for Elias more than he had for himself.

"You're better than I remember." Connor's avatar swung a sword at a fire-breathing dragon, making contact to gain twenty points, but lost fifteen when the creature's tail knocked him over.

Stu's character held his hands out and waved them, sending a sleep spell that mostly worked on the beast, and it got drowsy enough for Aiden's avatar to through a netting over it and tie it down.

"Yes!" Aiden punched the air. With the dragon down, the hoard in its cavern was split between the three heroes.

Connor kept punching buttons, grabbing a few loose scales that had fallen off the monster during the fight.

"Ok, c'mon. We need to get out of the cavern before it gets free" Stu punched a button and his character ran down the dark tunnel, a light extended from his palm, so he didn't activate any hidden traps. "Hurry. My hand lamp spell won't last forever."

Aiden and Connor followed, zig-zagging their way out when the rumblings started up again, signaling that the dragon was chasing them.

"We'll need to hide as soon as we get out." Connor had three scales in his arms, letting a fourth fall and not bothering to pick it up. It was too risky; the dragon might catch him if he stopped.

"I have an invisibility spell that I can use once we don't need the light." Stu panted, shifting his real body as he wove his avatar on the screen.

"Cool." Connor could speed up his character without the extra scale, so was able to keep up better. "How long will it last?"

"Not sure." Stu let his hand drop as the three avatars reached the opening into the forest. He pulled an icon from his belt bag and activated the invisibility spell; the three characters could only be seen by faint outlines, the graphic greenery seen through them.

"I hope it works." Aiden pulled a map from his belt bag and opened it so that it filled the screen. "Do we go back and buy the new weapons, or go sell the magic vendor the scales Connor grabbed?"

"I think we should get the weapons first; we might need them at the magic vendor." Connor squinted at the screen and the enlarged map, pointing at a spot marked with a red 'X'. "The weapons shop is closer, too."

"Stu?" Aiden nudged his friend.

"I agree. Let's do it." Stu nodded at the screen.

Aiden put the map away and the three headed down the path toward the 'X', the dragon left behind, snuffling the ground when it couldn't see them.

CHAPTER 10

"That was fun." Stu threw back the last of his beer and sighed. "It's been a while since I enjoyed a game that much."

Connor shot him a long, side glance, then looked to Aiden, a brow raised. "When did he start enjoying playing video games?"

"When he stopped focusing on football." Aiden snickered. "He found out he liked a lot of stuff better than football."

"Dude!" Stu punched his shoulder.

"What? Are you telling me I'm wrong?" Aiden wagged his bottle at him.

Groaning, Stu rolled his eyes. "I gained responsibilities."

Connor looked from one to the

other.

Stu sniffed and raised a middle finger at Aiden. "Connor, to fill you in, Stephanie got pregnant before I graduated, so I didn't go to college or play college football. Instead, I started working at her father's construction company and we got married."

"Elias?" Connor wasn't drinking, but tossed a pizza roll in his mouth.

"Yup. Elias." Stu took along breath. "Stephanie ended up just getting a GED after he was born and is now almost done with a nursing degree. When she's done, I'll start work on the harder engineering stuff; I already got all the lower level stuff done part-time."

"Huh." Connor stared at the platter of microwaved treats. "How did your dad take that?"

"Not good. He was really pissed for a while, but Mom dragged him to the wedding—it wasn't big, just a couple friends and some of Stephanie's family—and he got over the disappointment of me not playing football at college, but there's still some hard feelings that come out sometimes."

"I'm sorry."

Stu shrugged. "Stephanie and I are happy...and we have Elias. I have what I want; I don't need football."

Connor nodded. "I just finished a graphic design degree from a technical school. Not sure what I'm going to do with it, but I did well in my classes. I thought I'd go and get a Bachelor's, but I don't have the money, so I need to work before I can start on that."

Aiden didn't know what to say about his own education. His parents had put money away and done the prepay plan, so he was set for all four years. He'd gotten a couple of scholarships, too, which meant he didn't even have to work in the summer unless he wanted to.

"Aiden here's doing alright." Stu jabbed a thumb in his direction. "He's on track to graduate cum laude on time and everything."

"That's great." Connor grinned, slapping Aiden's shoulder. "What are you studying?"

"Computer programming. Minor in English."

"English?" Connor stared.

Aiden sighed. "Mom's request. She likes to write."

"Dude." Stu punched him again, gentler this time. "That's an understatement."

Hanging his head, Aiden whooshed a deep breath out. "Connor, when Mom had to close the child development center—happened right after you left—she

45

started writing children's books."

"Children's books?" Connor glanced at Aiden. "Is that a bad thing?"

"No," Aiden stood, stretching and putting the game controllers away, "it's just that she's been published."

"And?" Connor raised a brow in Stu's direction.

Stu chuckled. "Ever heard of Mercy Lacks?"

Connor nodded. "One of the kids in my foster home, Becky, loved her stuff. I think she had a copy of every books she'd written."

Aiden groaned.

"Are you saying Mercy Lacks is your mother?" Connor's voice cracked.

"Yeah." Aiden turned the X-Box off and looked at Stu. "You know it's past midnight, right?"

"Yeah." Stu stretched and yawned and stood. "That's why I only had the one beer, so I can drive home okay."

Connor still stared at Aiden, his mouth agape. "Jeez. Mercy Lacks is a big deal."

Aiden nodded. "Yeah. That's one reason we don't advertise that it's Mom."

"Wow." Connor grinned. "You're like, one degree from famous."

"Don't get me wrong, I'm very proud of her. It just gets awkward, sometimes, you know?" Aiden stared at Connor.

"Sure. I get it."

But Aiden had the feeling he didn't really.

Stu pushed Connor on the shoulder. "Where are you staying?"

"I figure I'll get a room at the Motel

8 out by the Interstate." Connor stood and yawned.

"No, you won't." Aiden shook his head.

"I won't?" Connor looked worried. "It's still there, isn't it? I checked the web site at the library before I came down."

"It's still there. But Mom won't be happy if you stay there. Not when there's a spare bedroom in the basement you can use." Aiden pointed at one of the three closed doors, two on one wall, the other just at the end in the corner.

Connor sighed. "Don't worry me like that."

Aiden beckoned. "Let's see Stu out, and grab your stuff from your car."

CHAPTER 11

Aiden knew the moment his parents arrived home at just before two a.m.; he was still awake.

It was almost too much knowing Connor was only one wall away.

He set his palm against the wall, the gray painted boards cool to the touch. The other twin bed, repurposed from his over-the-garage bedroom when his parents redid the house last year, was directly on the other side.

And Connor was sleeping in it.

The rooms were mirror images of each other, all the furniture from Aiden's childhood bedroom—two beds, two dressers, and two nightstands—had been repainted white and brought downstairs. His old bedroom now had a lovely double-bed with brass frame, a quilt made by the church group that Mom had won in a fundraising raffle, and a couple of ornate nightstands and a single dresser that matched.

Aiden hadn't minded. He was at school most of the time and sleeping in the basement bedroom when he was home offered a bit more privacy. His older sister, Jacey, and her husband, Rob, stayed in his old room when they visited; Jacey's room had been converted to a craft/writing room for their mother after her first book sold.

His parents were quiet, shuffling through the kitchen to the stairs, whispering and hushing each other as they went. Breakfast would be his responsibility in the morning; it was good that there were frozen waffles in the freezer.

Or, he could take Connor out for

breakfast. Since it was Sunday, most folx would be heading for breakfast late, and they would have the little pancake place in the strip mall mostly to themselves. The food was really good, and the owners friendly, so it was always a good place to eat.

And after, they could head into the comic shop next door, if Connor was still into comics, and check out what was new. Stu might enjoy playing video games now, but he still didn't see the draw of comics.

Of course, to do any of that, he'd have to get up in the morning, and to get up in the morning, he'd have to fall asleep. And he was having trouble doing that.

Turning in the narrow bed, he groaned. He couldn't shut his brain down. It wanted to go over every word Connor had spoken, every gesture made, every upturn of his lips, every crinkle at the corner of his eyes. It was worse than when he just spent time wishing he could see Connor.

A soft snore reverberated through the wall: Connor was asleep.

Somehow, that slight sound was reassuring. It meant that Connor was really there.

Aiden turned back over to the wall again, staring at the spot where he imagined Connor's head to be. If he concentrated, he could pretend he could see those blond curls nestled in a pillow, the mate to the blue blanket that covered him draped over his friend.

Closing his eyes, Aiden listened for the next snuffle, heard it again, and the images in his head subsided. His breaths deepened, and he fell asleep.

CHAPTER 12

Connor was already up and waiting on the basement family room sofa when Aiden stumbled from his bed and out into the world.

"Good morning." Connor grinned up at Aiden. "Bad night?"

Aiden shrugged. No way was he going to tell Connor the real reason he'd had trouble sleeping last night. "I didn't nod off until after I heard Mom and Dad get back." At least that wasn't a lie.

"When did they get in?" Connor frowned.

"Not until after two." Aiden sighed and sank down to the cushions on the other end of the sofa. He yawned and stretched, glancing at his phone to check the time. It was nearing nine a.m.

"Breakfast is on our own this morning. Do you want to risk my cooking or go out?"

Connor laughed. "Do you cook any better than I remember?"

Aiden cocked his heading, shooting a narrowed glare at his friend "No."

"Then I think I'd prefer to go out."

Grunting, Aiden got back up and trudged to his bedroom to get dressed. If they got out of the house and on their way soon, they'd still make it for breakfast before the after-church rush.

For the first time in a while, Aiden took care with what he wore, picking a shirt that had the least number of wrinkles and that wasn't baggy. He even tucked it into his black jeans and threaded a belt through the loops before rolling the sleeves up to his forearms. He didn't want to look too obvious.

When he came out of the bedroom,

pulling his dark hair back into a low but neat ponytail, the first hunger pangs had started.

Connor frowned at him. "Should I change?" He was wearing a t-shirt and jeans.

"No reason."

"You look dressed up." Connor stood and walked to his room. "Give me a minute."

Aiden regretted the time and care he'd taken. It hadn't been his intention to make Connor feel under-dressed. But he had. He hoped Connor didn't feel bad. There had been times in high school that Connor had only had a single t-shirt and jeans to wear that fit, and when others had mentioned it, he'd been embarrassed and ashamed.

Stu and Aiden hadn't cared what Connor wore, and still didn't. But Aiden may have messed that up.

Connor came out of the bedroom in the same jeans, but in a pale green polo that fit nicely to his shoulders. "I didn't bring a button-up, but this at least has a collar."

"You were fine as you were." Aiden wanted to make amends.

Shrugging, Connor said nothing.

"Well, let's go then. The first church services will be out soon, and Martin's will get busy." Aiden jogged up the stairs, waving for Connor to follow.

Connor did, though at a more thoughtful pace. "Is there someone there you're trying to impress?"

"What?" Aiden stopped at the top to spin around and stare at Connor.

"You're all dressed up." Connor pointed to Aiden's shirt and belt. "I thought maybe there's someone there, you know." He shrugged. "Never mind."

Damn. "No, Connor, there is no one that works at Martin's that I want to impress. Or that I like, or anything like that." Aiden took a steadying breath and entered the kitchen.

"Sorry." Connor's voice was low.

Fuck. Aiden grabbed his keys from the set of hooks next to the wall phone. "No reason to be sorry. I was snippy when I didn't need to be."

Connor was quiet walking out to Aiden's Mazda, and quiet on the drive to the restaurant, and quiet waiting for their table. They hadn't quite made it before the rush, so they had about a 10-minute wait standing just inside the door.

CHAPTER 13

It was awkward. Aiden wanted to apologize again, but wasn't sure what words to use. He'd snapped back, because Connor was a little too close to the reason for Aiden's attire—it just wasn't for the benefit of anyone who worked at the restaurant.

When they got their table—a small two-seater along the wall—Connor read over the menu in silence.

"They still have the best French toast." Aiden offered, trying to ease the gap in conversation.

Connor nodded.

Aiden sighed and thought about what he wanted to eat.

There was a tap on his hand.

He looked up to find Connor leaning over the table, a slight pink flush to his cheeks. "Are we paying Dutch?"

"My treat." Aiden grinned. "I'm the one who asked you."

Connor nodded and Aiden wanted to kick himself again. At the rate he was going, Connor wouldn't want to be friends anymore.

"Thanks." Connor bit a lip, his eyes scanning over the items.

"You can get whatever you want."

"Okay."

"I mean it."

Connor nodded. "I'll get the French toast, I think. With bacon."

"Sounds good." Aiden smiled. "I think that's what I'll get, too. Coffee?"

"Sure."

They set down their menus and

waited for the waitress to notice.

When the older woman made her way to their table, her eyes widened. "Connor Strayer? Is that you?"

Connor looked up. "Yes, ma'am."

"Well my goodness, look at you! How long has it been?"

When Connor didn't answer right away, the woman laughed. "You probably don't recognize me. Corina Winston, Sheila Winston's daughter. My mother lived in the mobile home park with your mom and dad."

Recognition hit Connor and he smiled. "Yes, sorry. It's been a few years." He held out his hand.

The waitress shook it and sighed. "All grown up and everything. How are you?"

"Pretty good."

"Visiting Aiden and Stu?" She flipped to a new page on her pad, and poised her pen over it, ready to take their order. "It's Spring Break, ain't it. Not in the mood for Florida?"

Connor's laugh held a hint of embarrassment. "I'm done with technical school, so no Spring Break for me."

She nodded and picked up the menus, repositioning her pen at the pad.

Aiden cleared his throat. "I'll have coffee—you can bring a carafe to the table, please—and the French toast with bacon."

Writing on the pad, she glanced to Connor.

"I'll have the same." He smiled.

"No home fries?"

Aiden raised a brow at Connor, who shook his head. "No, thank you."

"Just maple syrup or do you want a flavor? I think we have blueberry and peach this morning." She smiled at them but glanced at another couple coming through the door.

From the look on Connor's face, Aiden knew his preference for syrup hadn't changed. "The regular syrup is fine."

The waitress tapped the tabletop with the order pad and grinned. "I'll bring your coffee right out; the rest won't be long." Then she turned, scanning the dining room for a free table, then pointing to a four-seater along the far wall. "You can sit there, and I'll have someone come get your order."

CHAPTER 14

Breakfast was delicious, and they chatted about the food, the times they'd come in with Stu on a Saturday after football practice and he'd order two omelets and a high stack and eat all of it, the few times Connor had spent the night at Aiden's and they'd come in with his parents.

It was pleasant conversation, and Aiden pushed away the worry that he'd messed up.

When he paid the bill, Connor offered a five to include in the tip, and Aiden accepted, leaving an additional couple of ones to equal twenty percent of the bill.

"ComicStop?" Aiden asked once they were outside. The sun was warming the air and he really didn't want to go home yet. Maybe they could even go for a walk after, through the quiet downtown. Though he wasn't alone with Connor, it was just the two of them, and he wanted to make the most of it.

"Sure." Connor shrugged and followed Aiden down two store fronts to the small shop that sold comics, games, graphic novels, and items that went with them.

The little bell above the door pealed when they entered, and a red-and-blue haired teen called out a hello from behind the counter.

"Hey, Reese." Aiden waved a hand.

"Hey, Aiden. How's school?"

Aiden shrugged. "I'm hanging in there."

"You're on Spring Break, right?"

"Yup." Aiden walked to the front display. These were independent and self-published comics and art books, and he always tried to buy one whenever he came into the store.

Connor stood at his right elbow, looking around.

Aiden handed him a bright orange zine. "Check this out."

Accepting the book, Connor glanced over it, frowning. "What is it?"

"It's an indie. Made by Robert Malloy; you remember him? The geek that always won the computing and programming competition? He was a grade ahead of me and Stu."

"Oh, that's cool." And Connor flipped through to the first page, reading the story in pictures. "How much is it?"

"It's five bucks." Aiden touched Connor's hand when he went to set it back on the shelf. "But go ahead and read it; I always buy a copy. It's pretty good.

It's about a kid trapped in a computer and the adventures he has trying to get back out. Kind of like Tron, but not really."

While Connor read the twenty-four-page spread, Aiden looked over the rest of the items on the indie display, deciding on a couple more to purchase as well: another that he usually bought and a new one he hadn't seen before but was willing to read.

"Do you still read comics?"

Connor had always borrowed Aiden's or read them when he'd get to stay over and they weren't playing a video game.

"No." Connor shrugged and handed the zine back to Aiden. "My foster parents weren't into that kind of stuff, and I never really had money of my own to spend." He tapped the cover. "You're right, that is a pretty good story, though, and the art is well done."

They walked around the store, checking out the graphic novels more than the comics, and laughing at some of the art styles and how characters were posed.

Connor's knowledge of graphics and art was obvious, and Aiden could see how much he loved it.

And a nagging doubt entered his head. Connor was going to need a job, and soon. And that meant he'd be going to that job, might already have one.

And Aiden didn't know what to do about that.

CHAPTER 15

They were nearing the counter when someone called Aiden's name. He groaned. It was Melody Branden, a friend of Stephanie's from high school.

"Hi, Melody." He waved and set his items on the counter, turning to the cashier and hoping they got the hint that he wanted a quick transaction.

The kid got the silent message and rang everything up, not offering any insight on any other indie comic as they usually would.

"So, you're home on Spring Break, huh?" Melody sidled up to the counter, her eyes roving over Connor.

"Yup." Aiden handed a twenty over to Reese to pay for his purchase.

"Richie Daniels is having a party at

the lake tomorrow. It's open to anyone who wants to come." She leaned on the counter, smiling at Aiden.

"Sorry, I can't."

Melody pouted. "Why not? You never come to the parties."

Aiden wanted to roll his eyes and snap back that there might be a reason for that, but he didn't. He'd had this conversation with Melody, and a couple other folx from high school, before. "I'm helping my dad...with the garage." It was a good enough story; the garage always needed to be cleaned out.

"All day?" The sarcasm in her voice was enough to etch the wooden counter.

Reese handed Aiden the change from the twenty and the bag with the three zines in it. "Have a great day. Come back soon."

Aiden nodded and smiled. When he

turned, Melody was between him and the door.

"Hmm?" She raised a brow.

"No, but I'm home to help him with stuff. He had that heart attack last year, remember?"

The young woman narrowed her gaze. "That was last year. And I heard he's fully recovered."

Aiden sighed. He'd have to come up with a better excuse. "Sure, but we have to make sure he doesn't have a relapse, and we're doing some heavy lifting. The doctor still wants him to take it easy with that."

Melody huffed and turned her attention and wily smile on Connor. "How about you? Are you a friend of Aiden's from college?"

Connor blinked. "Um...friend, yes. From college, no."

"Well...the party?" Melody prompted, fluttering a hand.

"Um, no."

"Why not?" The hand landed on a jutting hip.

"Be...cause we're helping Aiden's dad clean out the garage?"

It sounded more like a question than a statement, even to Aiden, and he winced. Melody could be like a terrier if you weren't careful.

The young woman opened her mouth to keep talking at them, but the door opened and a female head popped in, followed by a hand holding up a bag from the beauty shop. "Hey, Mel. We're ready. Let's go."

Sniffing, Melody spun around and followed her friend.

Aiden sighed.

"That was a close call." Reese shook their head and leaned against the counter. "I usually duck in the back and let Hazel take over out here when any of that group come in."

Groaning, Aiden nodded. "I need to come up with a better excuse."

"Why do you need an excuse?" Connor frowned at the door.

"Because that one, and her cronies, won't let you say no, and will harangue you into the ground if you do." Reese leaned on the counter. "She almost got banned from the shop, but then she bought like a hundred dollar's worth of stuff and Greg decided not to."

They were all quiet for a moment; Aiden watching the parking lot to make sure Melody and her friends were gone before they left the store. Walking around downtown and running into her, or someone else, was not appealing.

"So," Reese broke the silence, "boyfriend?"

"Huh?" Connor flushed.

Reese giggled and stepped back. "Ah, you are." They winked at Aiden. "You do have an eye for handsome men."

Aiden flushed, too. "Uh, Reese-"

"Ooh." Reese pointed out the main window. "They're gone."

"Ah, right." Waving, Aiden backed to the door. "See you."

Connor waved, too, and followed Aiden out to the car. "Downtown?"

"You still want to?"

Connor shook his head. "No."

"Cool."

So they drove to Aiden's parents' house, stopping for four chocolate fudge sundaes—Connor's with banana slices on the side instead of peanuts—on the way.

"Four?" Connor held the tray on his lap.

"I can't come home with sundaes without one for Mom and Dad, too."

CHAPTER 16

The sundaes were greatly appreciated by the elder Mitchells, and the quartet relished them on the back patio, enjoying the early afternoon sun. Though it was warm for March, it wasn't quite warm enough for the canopy, so it stayed furled next to the house.

Aiden took the opportunity to let his father know they'd have to make a bit of a show of clearing out the garage, and asked if there were any other odd jobs that needed to be done.

"Hmm," Dad smacked his lips on some fudge sauce, "there's always the scrape and paint under the eaves that still needs attending."

Aiden nodded. "Do you have the stuff we need?"

"Yup, in the garage, somewhere..."

They all laughed, even Connor.

"I guess I'll be roped in to help, too?" Connor had eaten his bananas with the hot fudge and was now diligently working on the vanilla ice cream.

"Of course," Aiden snickered, "you used it for an excuse as much as I did."

"I had to agree with you, or your excuse wouldn't have worked." He tilted his chin up in a mock air.

Aiden groaned. "That is true. I guess I'll let you supervise, then."

"What am I supposed to do?" Dad was almost finished his sundae.

"You're supposed to be careful of your heart." Connor watched Aiden when he spoke.

Aiden sniffed. "I had to make it good, didn't I?"

Mom sighed.

"What's wrong, dear?" Dad turned to look at her, a bit of worry tinging his gaze. Aiden knew he worried that his Mom worried about his health too much since the scare last year.

She held up her empty cup. "My ice cream is finished."

Dad gulped down the last of his ice cream. "Well, I can't help you. Mine is gone, too."

Turning to Aiden, Mom batted her eyelashes at him. "Do you want the last of yours? I can reinforce the notion that your Dad needs to take it easy and extoll the virtues of our wonderful son who is willing to give up his Spring Break to keep his invalid father out of the hospital. It will also help me forget that you reminded me of your father's bad heart."

Aiden looked down at his cup; there was about a third of the ice cream left, along with a good dollop of the fudge sauce and the peanuts. He handed it over to his mother.

"Ah," Mom sighed—this one happy, "I do have a good son."

Connor looked at his rapidly melting ice cream then at Aiden. "You want some of mine that's left?"

"No, I'm good." Aiden chuckled. "If all goes as it has in the past, I wind up with an extra helping of my favorite part of dinner."

Connor snickered and gleefully finished his ice cream. "Well, I'm glad of that. I really like this sundae." He licked his spoon with a dramatic sweep of his tongue.

Which made Aiden flush. Standing, he collected the ice cream debris to take into the kitchen, keeping his head down to try to hide his embarrassment.

But Connor followed. "Hey, can we talk?"

Aiden shrugged. "Sure." The heat in his face was dissipating, so he felt safe bringing his head up to look at Connor.

"The kid at the comic shop thought I was your boyfriend?"

Shit. "Yeah. Sorry about that." Aiden felt the flush return." Reese knows I'm gay, so...I guess it was natural for him to ask me about you like that."

Connor bit his bottom lip.

Aiden thought he might burst if Connor didn't stop doing that stuff...but he couldn't say anything. It wasn't like his friend was doing it on purpose.

"You're gay?"

"I thought you knew? I mean..." Aiden cleared his throat and glanced to the backdoor. "There was my seventeenth birthday and all."

"I thought that may have been more about me than you." Connor glanced at the backdoor and frowned. "Your parents don't know?"

"What? Yeah, they know. That I'm gay. I just never told anyone...well, about that kiss." Aiden's cheeks were on fire.

Connor stared at him a moment, raising a finger to trace down Aiden's hot cheek. "Do you have a boyfriend? One that isn't me?"

Aiden shook his head. "No. I've been on dates, at university. And there was one guy, but..." He sighed and closed his eyes. "It didn't work out."

"Oh." Connor dropped his finger, shoving both hands in his pockets.

"I think," Aiden took a deep breath. He'd wanted to wait for this conversation, but it looked like he couldn't, "we need to head downstairs. There's something I need to tell you."

Connor frowned.

"Nothing bad, I don't think, but..." Aiden groaned. Why was this so hard? "Just, something you should know."

CHAPTER 17

They headed down to the basement, Connor first, Aiden second, making sure the door was shut behind him.

At the bottom of the stairs, Connor turned to look as him, and Aiden gestured to the sofa.

Connor sank down on one end, hands clasped in front of him, his knees bouncing.

Aiden took in a breath. "I'm the one who called CPS."

"What?" Connor whipped his head around to stare at Aiden.

"Your dad found out about the kiss—don't know how—and saw me walking home from..." Aiden frowned, he couldn't remember where he'd been that day, "wherever, and screamed out the window at me about what he was going to do to you, and to me, and gunned his engine and drove up on the sidewalk at me. I took off running, through backyards. I don't know how far I ran, I could hear him screaming still, from the road. Mrs. Smith-Williams saw me and grabbed me into her house. She helped me find the number and let me call from her house. First the sheriff, who wanted to ignore me, so she called her son-in-law in Johnstown, then we got the number for CPS and we called them. She let me stay there until Dad came for me."

"Fuck..." Connor closed his eyes and hung his head. "He found out from me. We were fighting and he said something about no one ever wanting a fucked-up runt like me. That I was just like my mother, worthless and unwanted...and it just came out. I said that I had you and I didn't need anyone else."

Aiden was silent, staring at Connor.

He'd never imagined that he had said anything. That he was the one who had told his father.

Connor sniffed and scrubbed a forearm across his face. "God, I'm sorry. Were you hurt?"

"No. I mean, some scratches from some bushes, that's all." Aiden reached out a hand, rubbing it over Connor's blond curls, tucking one behind his ear, trying to offer comfort. "I was mostly terrified of what might happen to you."

"They wouldn't let me call you. Or Stu. I did ask about him, too, or your parents, you know. Just to let you know I was okay." Connor looked away.

Aiden thought he might be crying.

They remained silent.

Finally, Connor cleared his throat. "Tell me about your boyfriend. The one that didn't work out."

84

"Jason," Aiden rubbed his fingers into his eyes, and sighed, "was a grad student, studying mathematics. We met in one of the labs; he was a student teacher. We ended up staying late one night—I had an exam and was struggling with something in calculus. He was nice and we got to talking and he asked me out for coffee and I said yes."

"Why didn't it work out?" Connor was watching his face, his green eyes dark.

"There was stuff he didn't understand." Aiden glanced at the old game box. "He thought I should just get rid of stuff that was old, even if it meant something important to me."

"Like what?"

Taking a deep breath, Aiden glanced at Connor, his gaze dropping to the floor. "He didn't understand why I wouldn't get rid of the old game box when I had a brand-new one."

"Why won't you?"

Instead of answering, Aiden stood up and walked to the switch, flipping the toggle to the game and turned it and the TV on. Picking up two controllers, he plugged them both in and handed one to Connor.

Connor took it, but frowned at it. "Aiden?"

"Just wait." He pressed a button, and the game came on the screen, the three player names flashing.

Do you want to continue the adventure?

Connor stared at the screen and tapped a button. The flashing words disappeared and faint music played. With a tap of the volume control, Aiden increased the TV sound so they could hear it better, and the game started playing—right where they'd left off all those years ago.

The pair played for an hour before Mom called down from the kitchen. "You two want some dinner? Dad's making burgers. From scratch."

Aiden raised a brow at Connor, who nodded and swiped with his avatar's sword, cutting the vines that covered a door they had to go through.

"Sure, Mom." Aiden's voice sounded like he had a bubble in his throat. "We're playing a video game, but we can pause it when its ready."

"Alright." And the door closed.

Half an hour later, they'd gone through the door, found a treasure chest with no key, found a map that showed where to find the key, scaled a mountain to reach the cave where the key was hidden, and were trying to answer the riddle to defeat the curse to earn the key

Gaymers

when Mom called down that dinner was
ready.

CHAPTER 18

Dad's home-made burgers were the best. He used mostly beef, but added a bit of sausage for flavor, and small chunks of cheese that got melty but not messy. There was more cheese, if you wanted it, and thick slabs of tomato and red onion to add.

And then, there was the brioche bun that Mom got from the bakery, uncooked and frozen, so she could pull four out to thaw and bake fresh for the burgers. She'd also made seasoned sweet potato fries, fresh cut and drizzled with olive oil and cooked until super crispy in the oven.

Connor stared at the table. "I kinda forgot how your Mom and Dad cook on Sundays." He didn't sound disappointed, though.

"I miss this when I'm at school."

Aiden waved for Connor to sit. "Mom, you need anything else put out?"

"The ketchup and mustard. No one takes mayo, right?" Mom set full plates in front of Dad and Connor.

Connor shook his head at the mayo question and licked his lips. "This looks really good."

Aiden set the condiments on the table and smiled when his mother set his plate in front of him; he had extra fries. He pointed at the mound of crunchy sweet potato strips. "See, Connor. This is what I get for giving up a bit of ice cream."

Laughing, Connor dressed his burger and drizzled ketchup over his fries. "That may have been a good trade. Next time, I might give up my ice cream if it means more of your Mom's fries."

Mom grinned, a faint blush of pink coloring her cheeks. "Keep that up and you might get extra without giving up your ice cream."

Connor elbowed Aiden, who laughed. "Guest privilege."

They ate dinner, the conversation sticking to memories of other Sunday dinners from Connor, and Dad and Mom recounting some of their more disastrous attempts at making special meals.

It was easy and Aiden almost forgot about his earlier conversation with Connor.

Then Dad asked them about what game they were playing.

Connor grew silent, swirling a glob of ketchup with a fry.

Aiden licked his lips and pushed his plate away. "A Crimson Journey."

Dad frowned. "That on the new game system?"

"Nope. It's one that we used to play

as kids. We're actually finishing the last game we were playing before..." he swallowed, "Connor left."

Those were lame words to describe what had happened. It sounded like he'd just left, like his family had moved away or he'd gone off to school.

"Is it one you play against each other or are a team?" Dad leaned back in his chair. Aiden forgot sometimes that, though his father didn't like to play the games with him, he talked about them because Aiden liked them.

His Dad had always been good like that.

Connor answered. "We're a team, trying to find our way to the Crimson Land of Prosperity." He chuckled. "It's easier, I think, to play without Stu."

Aiden snickered. "Too right, there. He usually dies pretty quick and we have to work to earn him a second—or tenth—

life."

Mom frowned. "Is this the one-"

"Yes." Aiden couldn't let her ask the question. He hadn't really explained fully about the game and the game box and Jason to Connor yet. They'd been concentrating on the game instead of talking.

And Aiden was mature enough to admit that he'd been happy to put off the discussion. It wasn't a particularly nice part of his history, and he hadn't been fair to Jason, and he didn't want Connor to think he always treated guys like that.

Connor's gaze slid to Aiden, but he didn't say anything. "It's a fun game. I kinda wish they made an updated version for the new systems."

"Why don't they?" Mom had taken the hint and said nothing more about which game it was, instead, following Dad's lead and just talking about the game.

Aiden shrugged. "They make new games."

"If they didn't make new games, there would be less reason to buy a new system." Connor set his chin in his hands, resting his elbow on the table. "I did an internship at a gaming company out of school until Christmas. That was my last quarter."

"Oh?" Aiden turned to look at Connor. "Was it fun?"

Connor wrinkled his nose. "Yes and no. I was assigned to a shoot 'em up war game and I don't like those kind of games, so I didn't like the games I was working on, and that was reflected in my work. My supervisor thought that was why I wasn't offered a job. He had me do some little touch ups and fixes on a fantasy game, and I did much better there."

"Shooting games are the big thing

now, eh?" Dad glanced at the coffee pot then checked the time. "Anyone want a cup of coffee in lieu of dessert?"

"Sure." Aiden figured they'd be playing the game for a while longer, and a bit of caffeine might be good.

"Yes, please." Connor stood with his plate and walked to the sink. "Do you want me to fill the dishwasher?"

Mom giggled. "No dear. I'll get it. Sit back down."

Connor left his plate in the sink and came back to the table.

Aiden leaned over and offered, in a stage whisper, "Mom is very particular about how her dishwasher gets filled."

"Ah," Connor nodded like he understood.

"So, what kind of job do you want?" Dad asked, pouring the water into the reservoir. "Marketing or advertising?"

Connor sighed. "I wanted a job in game design, like I interned at. I just couldn't make the internship lead into a full-time job. Probably for the best, since it would have been in New York city, and I don't like it there. Too crowded."

Dad nodded and pulled mugs out of the cupboard. He turned to Mom, "Miriam?"

"No thank you, dear."

He closed the cabinet door and set the mugs on the counter. "Aiden, do you want to get the cream and sugar?"

Aiden was already standing up when his Dad spoke, and headed to the fridge for the carton of creamer and the cabinet where the sugar bowl was stored. "You want a flavor syrup, Connor? Mom has vanilla and caramel...and it looks like a little bit of amaretto."

"Um...no thanks."

Aiden nodded and just brought the carton and bowl to the table. Though he might not have minded putting a syrup in his coffee, he could do without.

Dad set the three mugs on the table, sliding one over to Connor and the other across to Aiden.

Mom yawned and stretched. "You three can enjoy a little 'men's' talk. I think I'm going to bed."

Smiling, Dad tipped his face up for a kiss. "I'll fill the washer per specifications."

"Thank you dear. Much appreciated."

They talked jobs and pay and where Connor might be able to apply if he wanted to stay in St. Barnabby, or even Johnstown, and where he might be able to find an apartment and Dad offered the basement for room and board until he was settled and had some savings. Dad grabbed a pad of paper and a pen and wrote some of their ideas down.

In the end, they had a list of half a dozen places local, and another half dozen within a 100-mile radius. Dad had also jotted down resources like the employment office and the community college career center, as well as a couple of affordable apartment complexes and, of course, the basement.

Aiden stared at the list. He made a wish that Connor would get a job in town or at least somewhere close. And that he was good with staying in the basement for a while, at least. He didn't want to lose Connor to distance again.

CHAPTER 19

When Dad yawned, stretched, and stood to go to bed, he remembered the dishwasher.

"I got it, Dad." Aiden snickered.

"Don't forget the order for the plastics on the top shelf, and the order for the size of the plates on the bottom." Dad wagged a finger at him.

"I won't." Aiden stood and walked to the sink. "I'll make sure Mom can't tell it was me."

Dad frowned. "That makes it sound like you know how to load it per specs but just don't."

Aiden didn't say anything, just winked.

"Damn." Dad shook his head and

shuffled to the stairs. "Have a good night, boys; don't stay up too late. We need to tackle the garage tomorrow."

"Yes, sir." Connor saluted and stood, standing by the sink to watch Aiden fill the dishwasher. "Is your Mom really that picky?"

"It's an old machine." Aiden checked the size of the plates left in the sink. "If you aren't careful how you put stuff in, they don't all come clean."

"I'm usually in a rush, and don't pay enough attention to sizes or how dirty something is—the dirtier plates do better near the center." Aiden shuffled the plates on one side, then stared down with his hands on his hips, frowning. "What do you think?"

"I don't know." Connor tapped a plate. "That looks dirtier than the one behind it.

Aiden switched the plates. "There."

"Why don't you get a new one?"

"Jacey took up a collection from us kids and she's getting one for Mother's Day. Dad's in on it; he's paying for the install."

Connor chuckled. "And do you really mess up on purpose, so your Mom doesn't want you filling it?"

Aiden shrugged. "Not really. And that doesn't stop me from having to empty it, drying the stuff that's still wet, or handing washing the delicate stuff Mom doesn't trust it to not break."

"Are you going to be here for Mother's Day, to see her reaction?" Connor leaned against the counter, watching Aiden fill the detergent cup and close the door.

"Maybe. Depends on my exam schedule." He'd like to be here, not just to see his Mom get her new dishwasher, but to see Connor—if he was still here.

"What?" Connor nudged his shoulder, his voice low and gentle.

Aiden looked up. "Huh?"

"You looked all...not sad but...oh, what's the word...pensive, maybe?" Connor frowned. "You looked like you remembered something that worried you." He snapped his fingers. "You looked like you'd thought of something you didn't want to think about."

Damn. When did Connor get so insightful?

"Yeah, something I don't want to think about."

"About your Mom?"

"No." Aiden shook his head. "Not about my Mom."

Should he say it? Could he say it?

Aiden cleared his throat. "About you."

"Me?"

Aiden nodded and swallowed, then, in a raspy whisper, managed to get the words out. "I don't want to not see you again."

"Not see me again?" Connor stepped away from the counter, toward Aiden.

"I like that you're here. That we're spending time together. But..." he took in a deep breath, "when I go back to school, I won't see you. And..." another breath, "if you get a job somewhere far away, I won't see you again."

Connor just stared at Aiden, his green gaze directed straight into Aiden's brown one. "Aiden, I-"

"It's okay, Connor. Just because I feel like I do doesn't mean-" Aiden didn't get to finish his sentence.

Connor kissed him.

This one wasn't like the one all those years ago. That one had been shy and tentative, neither one of them really knowing what they were doing. Their teeth had clicked, their noses had bumped. They'd been embarrassed.

But now...Connor had gotten in some practice.

And so had Aiden.

They both knew to tilt their head, and how to tell which way the other intended to tilt first. Their lips were no longer tentative, but strong, sucking just a little, tongues joining in, touching, tasting.

Aiden moaned and reached his fingers through Connor's blond curls, shifting so their bodies aligned.

Connor wrapped his arms around Aiden's waist, his fingers gripping the material in the back of his shirt. His breathing quickened; he took long drags through his nose, the tempo meeting the thrust of his bottom lip pulling on Aiden's.

They broke apart.

"Connor?"

"You're why I came back, Aiden. If you don't want me to leave, I don't want to go anywhere." Connor's words were breathed into Aiden neck.

Aiden wrapped his arms around Connor, pulling him tight to him. "I want you here. Not necessarily in my parents' house, but I want you with me. I-" He pressed his nose into Connor's shoulder, squeezing him with his arms. "I'd like...I'd like to be with you. I want..." he took in a breath, "I'm pretty sure I love you, or almost do, and I'd like to love you like Mom and Dad love each other, and maybe...maybe make a life with you. You know...eventually."

Connor gripped him tighter. "Me, too. I want that, too. I mean, I know there isn't a guarantee or anything, but I'd like to work on it. When we're ready for that."

Sniffling, Aiden stood there, Connor in his arms, everything he'd every wanted right there. "Oh, God, yes. I want that. When I'm done with school and have a job and you're ready...I want that, too."

"So," Conner sniffle-snickered into Aiden's neck, rubbing his nose against the warm skin, "you want to continue the adventure?"

Aiden signed, nuzzling Connor's ear. "I want to win the whole game."

EPILOGUE

Five years later...

The small house mid-way down the street was freshly painted a pale green, with darker green shutters flanking the windows. The white picket fence circling the front yard looked friendly and inviting, the arched gate opening to an even brick walkway that led to the stained-wood front door.

Propped open, the door beckoned potential buyers to come inside.

Aiden parked the one-year-new, four-door Civic next to the 'For Sale' sign adorned with balloons and streamers, and raised a brow at Connor. "What do you think? It has a garage." He nodded at the single-car garage to the left of the house.

"Only a one car." Connor frowned

107

down at the listing in his hand. "This is the one for two-hundred thousand?"

"Yup. Everything's been redone, and it has a home warranty with it on all the work." Aiden turned the car off.

Connor sighed. "You want to go in."

"We should at least look at it. I mean, the last one had the garage we wanted, but the inside was horrible. I can handle parking my car outside."

Connor still owned the old Ford, albeit, he'd taken it to a shop and gotten it restored once he'd saved up the money.

"Fine." Connor opened his car door and got out, standing and stretching in the sun. "The front lawn looks nice."

Aiden nodded, walking around the front of the car, tapping the remote button to lock the doors. "Let's see what the inside looks like."

They walked through the gate,

Connor testing the hinges to see if they squeaked, and Aiden laughed at him, grabbing his elbow. "Come on. You're just getting cold feet."

"I just started freelancing, Aiden. What if I don't make enough money self-employed?" Connor looked up at the gingerbread trim that adorned the overhang of the wide front porch.

"I'm sure it will be fine." Aiden stopped them both, turning Connor to look at him. "You had a lot of clients lined up before you made this move. And if it doesn't work out right away, I make enough to pay the mortgage."

Connor opened his mouth to speak, but Aiden set a finger over his lips.

"The mortgage payment on this one would be less than what we pay in rent now."

Nodding, Connor closed his lips, flattening them into a line.

"You were the one who thought we should buy a house."

"I know, it's just..." Connor sighed and closed his eyes. "You're making it real and now...I'm worried."

"It's just a house Connor. If it doesn't work out, we sell it and go back to renting. Or live in Mom and Dad's basement." Aiden snickered and kissed Connor on the forehead. "Come on. Just because we're looking at it doesn't mean we have to buy it."

Inside the front door—which also didn't squeak—was a living area that stretched the width of the house, a fireplace on one end. The floor was a lovely, glossy light wood.

"This is nice." Aiden whispered, squeezing Connor's hand.

"Hi," a cheery female voice called from the kitchen, "welcome to 723 Windwood Lane. I'll be right out. There are refreshments in here if you like; iced tea and sugar cookies."

The owner of the voice moved toward them—there was an arch to the rest of the house in the wall at the end with the fireplace. Heels clicked on what looked like tile in a dining room, and then-

It was Melody Branden—well, Melody Smith-Williams now after marrying Mrs. Smith-Williams' grandson, Paul, from upstate New York. They'd moved back home after a couple years away. Paul now worked as an architect with Stu at the construction company.

The young woman sniggered and set her hands on her hips. "Well, at least now I know why you never said yes to my party invites."

Aiden sighed and rolled his eyes.

Connor laughed.

"Well, come on in." Melody waved a

hand for them to follow her, and moved back into the dining area. "This is a really nice starter home. Everything's been fixed and updated, with all the inspections available for you to look at. It has three bedrooms—one on the main floor with access to the downstairs bathroom/laundry combo, and two upstairs with another bathroom."

She turned back to them, spreading her arms wide. "This is, of course, the formal dining room. It is a bit on the small side, but it has built in cabinets in two corners," she pointed to each corner cabinet, "and a modern light fixture," she pointed up.

Spinning around, she led the way to the kitchen. "The kitchen is large, with an eat-in space in front of the window for a dinette set. All the appliances are brand new and the warranties transfer with the house."

"Downstairs bedroom is there," another pointed finger, indicating a small hall beside the stairs leading up, "and that door is the main access to the bath and laundry. Go on upstairs if you want and look around. There's a full half-acre lot, the one-car garage, back patio and shed." Melody squinted at a wall. "I think that's it for my spiel. Let me know if you have any questions."

Upstairs, Connor was quiet, and Aiden started to worry that it was too much. Then...

"Let's do it." Connor grabbed his arm.

"What? Here?"

"Let's buy this house." Connor grinned at him and punched his arm, rubbing the spot after.

"You sure?" Aiden found Connor's hand with his fingers and squeezed.

Connor nodded. "Yeah. For some reason...I don't know, this feels right, you know?"

Swallowing a sudden lump in his throat, Aiden bent down and kissed his husband. "Yeah, I know."

Connor kissed him back, then pulled away. "Time to start a new adventure?"

"This first of many." And Aiden wrapped his arms around the love of his life and let out a happy sigh, looking into one of the upstairs bedrooms, painted in pastels with a rainbow on one wall. "Let's continue with this adventure forever."

End

Like what you read? Want more?

Check out Waiting for Normal, available from www.dreampunkpress.com, Amazon, or your local favorite bookseller.

DreamPunk Press

Made in the USA
Middletown, DE
30 March 2024